DREAMWORKS

SHE-RA
AND THE
PRINCESSES OF POWER

ISLAND OF MAGICAL CREATURES

BY TRACEY WEST

ILLUSTRATED BY HEDVIG
HÄGGMAN-SUND

SCHOLASTIC INC.

ISBN 978-1-338-29843-7

10 9 8 7 6 5 4 3 2 1   19 20 21 22 23

Printed in the U.S.A.   23

First printing 2019

Book design by Carolyn Bull

CONTENTS

The World of Etheria IV

Chapter 1: Into the Woods 7

Chapter 2: The Princess Council 19

Chapter 3: An Ancient Mural 29

Chapter 4: Eyes in the Darkness 39

Chapter 5: Across the Ice Bridge 47

Chapter 6: Battle on the Gorge 53

Chapter 7: Arcana Island 63

Chapter 8: Twinkles the Mighty 69

Chapter 9: Following Treeleaf 83

Chapter 10: Catra's Back! 97

Chapter 11: Decisions 109

Chapter 12: A Bond at Last? 117

THE WORLD OF
ETHERIA

On the planet Etheria, the kingdom of Bright Moon is recovering from a big battle.

It began when the Horde drained the power from the runestones that lend magical protection to the rebel kingdoms and their princesses. Bright Moon was the last to fall. Led by She-Ra, the princesses joined forces in Bright Moon and learned that when they are together, their powers are stronger. They restored power to the Moonstone protecting the kingdom and defeated the Horde troops.

Even though they are victorious, there is no time for the princesses to celebrate. Their kingdoms are in ruins. Horde robots still roam the Whispering Woods, attacking anyone who crosses their path. And Adora knows that her old friend Catra will not rest until the Horde rules Etheria. Their next attack could happen at any time.

Now Adora and the princesses must figure out their next move, while Adora must find her place in the world of the princesses. Will she ever learn why she was destined to become She-Ra? Will she be able to help Catra see the light? And when will she stop saying the wrong thing to Swift Wind, her magical flying horse?

As her story unfolds, meet her and some of the characters who will help determine her fate . . .

ADORA

Raised by the Horde, Adora believed she was doing good. But when she finds a mythical sword that unlocks her power as She-Ra, Adora is driven to fight for Etheria as a leader of the Rebellion.

ABILITIES: Adora is a clever problem solver, a fast and athletic soldier, and a brave fighter.

SHE-RA

When Adora raises her sword and pledges to fight "for the honor of Grayskull," she is transformed into the mythical warrior princess She-Ra. Adora retains her personality and sense of self, but she's taller and stronger—and has much better hair.

POWERS: Super-strength, shape-shifting sword, limited healing powers, connection to the ancient First Ones of Etheria

THE HORDE

CATRA

Catra and Adora were both orphans and were close growing up in the Horde; they thought of themselves as sisters. Catra is a prankster with a villainous streak that she is forced to explore once Adora discovers the sword.

ABILITIES: She's cunning and fast, with catlike reflexes.

SCORPIA

A Force Captain in the Horde, Scorpia is Catra's new best friend (or, at least, Scorpia thinks she is). She is technically a princess of the fallen Scorpion Kingdom, which Hordak took over years ago.

POWERS: Poisonous scorpion tail and above-average strength

HORDAK

The evil leader of the Horde is bent on world domination. The Horde recruits rarely see him, as he prefers to plot from the depths of his lab.

ABILITY: He has a brilliant technological mind.

THE REBELLION

GLIMMER

The princess of Bright Moon is driven to find her own path and is an enthusiastic leader of the Rebellion. She has inherited magical powers from her mother, but her magic is limited, which can make her feel insecure at times.

POWERS: Teleportation, energy blasts, sparkle powers

BOW

Glimmer's best friend is a good guy who values loyalty and honor above everything else. He will do anything for his friends— and even complete strangers.

ABILITIES: He's an expert archer and a whiz with technology.

QUEEN ANGELLA

She is Glimmer's mother and the immortal queen of Bright Moon. After the tragic death of her husband at the hands of the Horde, she is overprotective of her ʾughter.

ʾ: Flight

SWIFT WIND

He was an ordinary horse until Adora accidentally transformed him with She-Ra's sword. He quickly became a valuable asset to the Rebellion.

POWERS: Flight, speed, and he can talk!

PERFUMA

She is the peace-loving ruler of the kingdom of Plumeria. While she is happiest when things are in perfect harmony, she is strong and not afraid to fight for what is right.

POWERS: She controls and grows plants and flowers.

MERMISTA

Although she's not quick to show her real feelings to others, Mermista has a soft side when it comes to her friends. And if you want to know the truth about something, Mermista will tell you without sugarcoating it.

POWERS: She controls water, and her legs can transform into a fishlike tail.

FROSTA

Because she's the youngest of the princesses, Frosta sometimes puts on a tough exterior to earn the respect of her subjects in the Kingdom of Snows. She's got awesome powers and is not afraid to use them.

POWERS: She controls ice and snow.

NETOSSA

She's dependable and always shows up with Spinnerella when the Rebellion needs help. She gets defensive when her powers are questioned, because she knows that her nets can take down almost any opponent.

POWERS: She conjures up energy nets that can trap objects of all sizes.

SPINNERELLA

She's kind and sweet, but just like the wind, she can go from breezy to stormy in a heartbeat. Like Netossa, she has always been loyal to the Rebellion.

POWERS: She controls the wind, creating cyclones that blow her enemies away.

CHAPTER 1
INTO THE WOODS

"Swift Wind, circle back!" She-Ra yelled.

"Why are we going back?" the flying horse asked. "There's nothing there!"

"I thought I spotted something moving," She-Ra replied. The princess clung to his orange mane with one hand and held her sword in the other. Her long, blonde hair streamed behind her.

Swift Wind snorted and then quickly changed course, his rainbow-colored wings pushing against the air currents. Then he soared across the Whispering Woods, the thick forest surrounding the kingdom of Bright Moon.

She-Ra scanned the trees, searching for signs of a Horde robot. Just a few days ago, the Horde had attacked Bright Moon and had almost won. But the princesses of Etheria had banded together and defeated the Horde army. The army had retreated, but some of the Horde robots were still roaming the woods.

"Down there!" She-Ra cried. "Can we get closer?"

"Does a duck quack?" Swift Wind asked, and he dove down toward the treetops.

"I don't know, does it?" She-Ra asked. "A duck is a furry—no, it's a bird, right? The kind that swims on ponds? Is quacking like swimming?"

Swift Wind snorted. "Didn't they teach you *anything* in the Fright Zone?"

She-Ra wanted to point out that it wasn't her fault that there were no cute animals in the Fright Zone and that she was doing her best to learn about them. But there was no time for that. Now she could clearly see the robot they'd been pursuing.

Horde robots had always reminded her of giant,

four-legged spiders. The robot's brain and weapons center was a metal globe perched on top of the legs. This one crashed through the underbrush, the red eye on the globe moving back and forth, searching for humans.

"We need to get closer," She-Ra said.

"I've got to stay above the trees," Swift Wind countered.

"Why?" She-Ra asked.

"I need room to flap my wings," he reminded her. "That helps with the whole flying thing."

"Fine, we'll flush it out," She-Ra said.

She aimed her sword at the bot. Blue energy shot down and zapped it. Its eye swirled up and saw She-Ra.

"Fly ahead, to the clearing!" She-Ra instructed Swift Wind.

The horse obeyed, speeding over the woods, and the robot followed in pursuit below. They reached the clearing at roughly the same time, and the bot began barraging She-Ra and Swift Wind with red laser blasts.

"Hey, watch the tail!" Swift Wind complained, flying up to dodge the blast. "She-Ra, can you do something about this guy?"

She-Ra aimed her sword at the robot again, and this time she had a clear shot. She aimed right for the robot's prime target: its laser eye.

Zap! The blue blast from her sword hit its mark, sending sparks shooting from the robot. One of its legs collapsed.

"Finish it!" Swift Wind cried, swooping down over the robot. She-Ra reached down and sank her sword into the top of the dome. As she pulled it out, more sparks flew.

"Nice!" the horse said.

Sparking and smoking, the Horde robot collapsed. The laser eye dimmed and went out.

"Yes!" She-Ra cheered.

Swift Wind gracefully landed in the clearing, and

She-Ra climbed off his back. She transformed into Adora, her usual form. While She-Ra was an eight-foot-tall legendary princess with superhuman powers and epic hair, Adora was an average-sized young woman with sharpened battle skills and hair pulled back in a sensible ponytail.

"Back to Adora already?" Swift Wind asked. "There could be more robots out there."

"We can go robot hunting later," she replied. "There's a meeting of the Princess Council in a few minutes, and I need to be there."

"She-Ra *is* a princess," Swift Wind said.

"Yeah, but I fit in the chair much better than she does," Adora said. She began walking toward Queen Angella's palace, and Swift Wind followed.

"Can I come to the meeting, too?" he asked.

"I don't think so," she replied. "I think it's a princess-only thing, and you're, you know, a flying horse."

"Bow isn't a princess, and *he* gets to go," Swift

Wind pointed out. "Also, I'm part of the Rebellion! And if I can't hang out with the princesses, who can I hang out with?"

Adora shrugged. "What about other horses?"

Swift Wind snorted. "In case you haven't noticed, I am not like other horses. I am the only magical, flying, talking horse in Bright Moon! Regular horses just don't get me. I've been trying to start a revolutionary movement to convince them to leave their masters and be free. But they're content to eat hay in their warm, cozy stables." He shook his head.

They had crossed into the village and were passing a barn with a fenced-in field. A brown horse stood by the fence, munching on a hay bale.

Swift Wind stopped in front of her.

"Hear me, sister! Break free of the chains of servitude that bind you and join me in the glorious freedom of revolution!"

Neeeeeeeigh, the horse whinnied in reply.

"What did she say?" Adora asked.

"She said it's Alfalfa Tuesday at the farm, and she's been looking forward to it all week," Swift Wind said. "Such a shame. She is a puppet of her overlords!"

He flapped his wings. "I'll see you at the castle, Adora!" he said, and then he flew off.

"Hey! Can't I get a lift?" she called after him, but he didn't turn back.

Adora sighed and continued her walk. She looked around, marveling at how happy and peaceful the kingdom looked. During the battle of Bright Moon, it had been plunged into darkness. The Horde had found a way to attack the Moonstone, the magical runestone that protected the kingdom and gave Queen Angella and Princess Glimmer their powers. For one scary moment, Adora had been sure that Bright Moon would be lost forever.

Catra had been sure of it, too. Catra had been her best friend when they were growing up in the Fright Zone together, trained to become soldiers of the

Horde. Then Adora had found the Sword of Protection and transformed into She-Ra. She'd met Glimmer and Bow and realized that everything she'd learned in the Fright Zone was a lie. So Adora had joined the princesses, and Catra had become a force captain in the Horde—and her sworn enemy.

Adora reached up to touch her cheek. The mark was gone, but she could still feel where Catra had scratched her with her sharp claws during the battle. She could still hear Catra's cruel taunts inside her head.

It won't be over until your friends find out that you've failed—that you were too weak to save them.

Catra hadn't counted on the power of the princesses, and how strong they could be. Adora still got chills, thinking about all the powerful energy she had felt when the princesses had banded together. It had filled her with more hope than she'd ever known—a feeling that no matter what the princesses faced, they could overcome it.

That powerful energy had been too much for Catra. She and the Horde army had retreated, but Adora knew that Catra wouldn't stop until she'd defeated the princesses for good.

Part of her still hoped she could get through to Catra and bring her over to the princesses' side.

That will never happen, she argued with herself. *She is too filled with hate. Too loyal to the Horde.*

And then a thought chilled her. What if she had never found the sword? She would have been the one leading the charge against Bright Moon, with Catra by her side. There would have been no She-Ra to defend the kingdom. In that scenario, the Horde would have won, and Bright Moon would have been lost . . .

"Adora!"

Glimmer appeared in front of her in a shower of

pink sparkles. The sparkles settled into her pink-and-purple hair.

"You're late for the meeting!" Glimmer said.

"I know, but there was this robot, and then Swift Wind . . ." Adora began.

"No time!" Glimmer said. She hugged Adora, and *poof!* They transported in a glittery cloud.

CHAPTER 2
THE PRINCESS COUNCIL

Adora and Glimmer appeared in the Princess Council's meeting room in a shower of sparkles. The other princesses were already there.

Perfuma had her eyes closed with her palms pressed together in front of her face. Dark pink flowers were scattered in her long, pale hair.

Mermista was twirling a strand of her aqua blue hair around one finger, yawning.

Frosta, the youngest princess, was impatiently drumming her fingers on top of the big, round meeting table.

Netossa and Spinnerella had their heads together, whispering.

Besides the princesses, there was Bow, Glimmer's best friend. And sitting tall and looking over them all was Queen Angella. Her pale pink wings fascinated Adora. They were so pretty, but also so powerful. Adora had seen the queen fly with the speed of an eagle during the battle of Bright Moon.

"I found her!" Glimmer announced to the group.

"Sorry I'm late," Adora said. "I was taking down a Horde robot in the woods."

At that moment, Swift Wind walked into the room. "You mean *we* took down a Horde robot," he corrected her.

"That's what I meant," Adora said. "But you weren't in the room—never mind."

"Will you be staying for the meeting, Swift Wind?" Queen Angella asked him.

"Of course I am. I'm a member of the Rebellion, aren't I?" the horse replied.

Queen Angella raised an eyebrow, but didn't argue. She turned to Adora.

"What is your report from the Whispering Woods?" she asked.

"There are still more robots wandering the woods—at least a dozen," Adora replied.

"I don't understand. I thought the Horde army retreated," Spinnerella said.

Adora nodded. "They did, but it was a hasty retreat, and they didn't have time to gather all of their bots."

"That's right! We sent them running!" Frosta cheered. "I was all, like, *pow!* And then Glimmer was, like, *zap!* And then Spinnerella came in with a *whoosh!* It was awesome."

"We definitely won the battle, but I know the Horde," Adora reminded them. "They are not going to let this one defeat stop them. They'll be back for another round. And this time, they'll have a different plan."

"And we'll be ready for them," Glimmer said confidently.

"We need to make sure that we are," Adora replied. "The Horde has even more troops and more robots than they brought to the battle. If they hit us with everything they've got, we could be in trouble."

"Even with Princess Power?" Frosta asked.

Adora nodded. "Even with Princess Power. So I thought today we could brainstorm. What can we do to increase our strength? Or improve our strategy?"

Perfuma's eyes fluttered open. "Did the meeting start?"

"Yes, Adora's been saying, like, a whole bunch of stuff," Mermista said. "Weren't you listening?"

"I was grounding and centering to prepare for the meeting," Perfuma answered with a smile. She looked at Adora. "What was the question again?"

"What can we do to make the Rebellion stronger?" Adora asked.

Netossa spoke up. "They've got soldiers. Maybe we need soldiers."

"I love that idea," Spinnerella said. "We could travel to the villages around Etheria and recruit people."

"That's not a *bad* idea," Adora said, "but Horde soldiers go through years of conditioning. We'd have to set up some kind of training camp."

"Only Adora and myself have the necessary background to train soldiers," Queen Angella reminded everyone.

"Hey, I'm self-taught," Glimmer said. "I could do it. And don't forget Bow. He's a master with a bow and arrow."

Bow nodded. "We could mass-produce my trick arrows."

"My Snow Guards could help, too," Frosta chimed in.

"And Netossa could teach our soldiers how to toss nets," Spinnerella said. "They wouldn't be magical nets, like hers, but nets can still be useful."

"That's right!" Netossa agreed.

Mermista frowned. "I don't know. Regular people can't learn princess stuff, can they?"

"They don't need to learn princess stuff," Perfuma said. "When the Horde was attacking Plumeria, Adora, Bow, and Glimmer inspired the people of my kingdom to fight back. They did a great job!"

"They did," Adora agreed. "But that was just a small group of Horde soldiers that day. I'm just not sure we could compete against the whole Horde army."

"Adora's got a point," Frosta said. "We need something special that the Horde doesn't have, like our Princess Power."

She gazed around the room, stopping at Swift Wind. "Like Swift Wind! Imagine if we all had talking, flying horses like him! The Horde would never stand a chance against us."

"I'm flattered, Frosta, but you know that I'm one of a kind," Swift Wind said. "I'm the only talking, flying creature on Etheria, thanks to Adora's sword."

"It's a nice thought, Frosta, but it's not very practical," Adora said.

Queen Angella spoke up. "It's quite possible that Swift Wind is not the only magical creature on Etheria," she said.

Swift Wind looked surprised. "What do you mean?"

"Just outside the kingdom, there are the remains of a First Ones building with an interesting mural on it," the queen explained. "It shows an island of animals. Scholars who have tried to translate the wall think that these creatures might have magical powers. They might not be flying horses, but maybe they could be helpful. I believe that Frosta's idea has some merit."

Frosta beamed. "I knew it!"

"Magical creatures?" Adora asked. "You mean like the Elementals?"

Adora had fought her share of Elementals before. They guarded First Ones sites all over the planet.

They were dormant until they detected intruders—and then they attacked.

Queen Angella shook her head. "No, they appear to be magical versions of ordinary Etherian creatures," she replied.

Bow piped up. "Adora can read First Ones language," he said. "We should go to the mural and check it out."

"I'll go, too," Glimmer offered.

"I like this plan!" Swift Wind said. "Imagine if there really *is* an island of magical creatures somewhere. Maybe they'll join my cause and help me liberate the animals of Etheria!"

"That's a nice idea, Swift Wind, but before we can free your horse friends, we've got to defeat the Horde," Adora pointed out.

"*Nice* idea? Seriously? Is that what you think of my life's work?" Swift Wind asked. "It's really important to me, Adora."

"I know that!" Adora shot back. "I know it's important. It's just that—" She sighed. Why did everything she say to Swift Wind always come out wrong?

"So are we going to find the island, or not?" Frosta asked.

Adora turned to the queen. "Bow, Glimmer, and I will go to the mural and come back with a report."

"And Swift Wind," the horse added.

"You're always included. I just meant—" Adora sighed again. "*And* Swift Wind."

Queen Angella nodded. "Excellent. I'll get you a map showing the location of the ruins. While you do that, the rest of us will further discuss the recruitment initiative."

Bow jumped up. "The Best Friend Squad is on it!"

CHAPTER 3
AN ANCIENT MURAL

"Guess I'll fly ahead and meet you guys there," Swift Wind said.

Adora grinned and held up a rolled-up piece of paper. "Not this time," she said. "*I've* got the map."

"Hmph. Walking's no fun when you can fly," Swift Wind muttered.

"Yeah, when I lost my powers, it was so frustrating not being able to teleport," Glimmer said. "But I like walking because then I get to spend time with my friends."

Friends. It made Adora happy every time she realized she had made so many friends since she'd left the Horde. She counted Swift Wind as one of them, although the two of them still hadn't bonded yet. She knew that as much as Swift Wind liked his transformation, it had been a real shock to him, and he was still trying to get used to it.

"Anyway, it's not far to the ruin," Adora said. "It's just a little farther to the east."

"Fine," Swift Wind said, and with a swish of his orange tail, he trotted ahead of them.

"He really is an amazing horse," Glimmer remarked, watching him.

"Yeah, he's the best," Bow agreed.

"I know," Adora said. "It's just . . ."

"Just what?" Glimmer asked.

Adora lowered her voice. "I haven't figured out how to really work with him yet. When I'm riding him, we need to work together. But when I want to go right, he wants to go left."

"Kind of like me and Glimmer," Bow remarked.

Glimmer's purple eyes flashed. "What do you mean?"

"Well, we're different," Bow said. "You're messy, and I'm neat. You flip out easily, and I'm pretty chill. You're loud, and—"

"Okay, I get it," Glimmer interrupted him. "What's your point?"

"My point is that we're best friends. We have a bond. So none of those things matter. When we team up, we can do anything," Bow said.

"Aw, that is so sweet!" Glimmer said, hugging his arm.

"Yeah, sweet," Adora said absently, glancing up at Swift Wind. *Will we ever be a great team, like Bow and Glimmer?* she wondered. *Will we ever bond?*

That's when she saw the blinking red light up ahead on the forest floor.

"Swift Wind, stop! Stop!" she yelled, running toward him.

Swift Wind stopped and turned back to her. "What now?"

Adora stepped in front of him and pointed behind her. "That red light—it's a Horde laser grenade. It must have dropped off one of their tanks when they retreated."

"Can we disarm it?" Bow asked.

"They're tricky," Adora said. "I know a safer way."

She slowly approached the weapon—a blinking red light embedded in a metal dome the size of an apple. Holding her breath, she picked it up—and then she tossed it as far as she could.

BOOM! The explosion rocked the forest, moving the earth under their feet.

"*That* was the safest way?" Bow asked.

Adora shrugged. "Everyone's okay, right?"

Her friends nodded.

"Thanks, Adora," Swift Wind said. "I might have stepped right on that thing."

"You're welcome," Adora replied.

"Although it proves my point. Flying is better than walking!" the horse added.

"Walking is safe, if you look where you're going," Adora muttered.

"I'm sorry, did you say something?" Swift Wind asked.

"Nothing," Adora replied. "You're right. Flying is better than walking sometimes. And sometimes walking is better. Like if you want to sneak up on somebody."

"Who are we trying to sneak up on?" Swift Wind asked.

"Nobody," Adora replied. "I just meant—"

Glimmer interrupted her. "Adora, are we almost there?"

Adora looked at the map. "It's not much farther now."

They continued through the woods for a few minutes more, and then they saw it: the crumbling remains of a circular First Ones building.

"Any sign of Elementals?" Bow asked.

"This place is small," Adora said, drawing her sword. "But if any show up, I'll be ready."

They stepped inside. Adora felt a slight chill go up her spine, as it did every time she entered a First Ones building. Sunlight streamed through cracks in the ceiling, lighting up the walls. They were overgrown with vines, but the lines of the mural peeked through them. Adora began to pull away the plants, and Glimmer and Bow helped.

"Wow!" Glimmer exclaimed.

The ancient painting depicted what definitely looked like an island, covered with trees and flowers. There were animals drawn all over it. At first glance, they looked like regular animals, but as the friends looked closer, they began to notice strange details.

"That sloth there looks like it's floating," Bow remarked, pointing.

"And that porcupine looks like it's doing martial arts," Glimmer added.

"I don't see any flying horses, though," Swift Wind remarked.

Adora scanned the scene until she found First Ones writing scrawled across the bottom. It looked like a bunch of strange symbols, but when Adora held the sword and looked at the words, they made sense in her head.

"'The energy on Arcana Island has had a strange effect on the creatures there. They have all developed unusual powers,'" Adora read aloud.

"*Unusual* powers? That doesn't sound so impressive," Swift Wind remarked. "Maybe the animals are just weird."

"The word in the First Ones language can mean the *good* kind of unusual, too," Adora pointed out. "Just like you're a good kind of unusual."

Swift Wind frowned. "You think I'm unusual?"

"In a *good* way," Adora repeated. "I mean, you've got awesome rainbow wings! And you can talk. That's unusual, right?"

Glimmer spoke up. "This island sounds promising. But how do we get there?"

Bow pulled away some more vines. "Check it out! I think this is a map."

He was right. It was a map of Etheria, with an island painted gold in the middle of a large lake in the southeast.

Bow used his tracker device to snap a picture of the map. "Got it!"

"Great!" Adora said. "I think we got what we came for. Let's go report back to Queen Angella."

They hurried back to the castle, and Adora gave the report.

"Unusual animals?" Mermista repeated. "Doesn't that mean they're just weird?"

"That's what I said," Swift Wind said.

"The First Ones word I translated can mean *good*

unusual. Like extra strong or powerful," Adora replied.

"This is worth pursuing," Queen Angella said. "But we still have Horde robots roaming these woods. Some of us will have to stay behind to deal with them."

Frosta's hand shot up. "I want to go to the island!"

"Spinnerella and I don't mind staying," Netossa replied.

"Sure," Spinnerella agreed. "I'll blow down the robots with my wind powers, and Netossa can stop them in their tracks with her magical nets."

"Excellent," Queen Angella said. "Mermista, Frosta, and Perfuma, you can accompany Adora, Glitter, Bow, and Swift Wind to Arcana Island."

"All right!" Swift Wind cheered. "Let's go put together an army of magical creatures!"

CHAPTER 4
EYES IN THE DARKNESS

"What are those things the Horde flies around on?" Glimmer asked. "Skiffs?"

Adora nodded. "That's right. Skiffs."

"Bright Moon needs to get some of those," Glimmer said. "We've been walking forever!"

"This is why we all need our *own* magical creatures," Frosta said. "Then we could all fly around like Adora and Swift Wind." She paused and turned to Adora. "Why aren't you flying there ahead of us?"

"Because princesses need to stick together," Adora said firmly.

"Princesses and their friends," Bow added.

"Of course! And their friends," Adora agreed.

"I don't mind walking," Perfuma said. "Walking is good for the mind and spirit as well as the body. And I'm seeing plants I've never seen before! Isn't that flower beautiful?" She pointed to a red bloom growing by a tree.

Bow reached down and plucked it out of the ground. "Here you go," he said, handing it to her with a smile.

She held up her hand to stop him. "It's called Poison Peony, Bow," she said. "You might want to put it down. It's beautiful, but dangerous."

"*Ahhhh!*" Bow tossed the flower aside. "Thanks for the warning."

Mermista yawned. "Are we going to, like, camp out or something? It will be dark soon."

Adora nodded. "Sure. We'll make camp in the next clearing we see."

"Camping, yes! It'll be like an outdoor sleepover," Frosta said.

"We'll have to take turns keeping watch," Adora told her. "There could be Horde soldiers out here."

"I'd be surprised," Glimmer remarked. "We're far from Bright Moon. The Horde hasn't been spotted in this part of Etheria for years."

"The Horde hadn't attacked Bright Moon for years, either," Adora reminded her, and Glimmer's face darkened. "Sorry. We just need to take precautions."

About an hour later they reached a clearing and began to set up camp.

"Look, wild mint!" Perfuma cried. "I'll make us some tea."

"I'll find some water," Mermista offered.

By the time the sun set, they were all seated on bedrolls around a crackling campfire, eating rations they'd brought with them from Bright Moon and drinking Perfuma's tea.

"I still don't believe what Bright Moon rations

are," Adora remarked, looking down at her plate. "Cookies? Fruit? Sandwiches in the shape of bunnies?"

"And I can't believe that you used to eat gray food bars all the time," Glimmer shot back.

"Sometimes they were green. Or brown," Adora said. "But don't get me wrong. Bright Moon rations are way better!"

Bow yawned. "It's been a long day. We should go to sleep soon. Want me to take first watch?"

"I'll do it!" Frosta offered, but she yawned, too.

"I'm not sleepy yet," Adora replied. "I've got it. I'll wake Bow up in two hours, and you can take third watch, Frosta."

"I'll do the watch with Frosta," Glimmer offered, and Frosta smiled. "Wake me up, too, Bow."

"I'll try," Bow said. "But waking you up isn't easy. Remember that time I had to dump ice water on you?"

"I do, and I am still planning my revenge," Glimmer answered. "Don't worry. I'll wake up."

Adora turned to Swift Wind. "Do you want to keep watch with me?" she asked, hoping he would say yes. Maybe with some time alone, the two of them could finally begin to get to know each other better.

"Sure," Swift Wind said, but then he opened his mouth and gave the biggest yawn Adora had ever seen. She noticed that his eyes were drooping.

She patted his head. "Never mind, Swift Wind," she said. "Get a good night's sleep."

"Thanks, Adora," Swift Wind replied, and he gratefully sat down and closed his eyes.

A short while later, Adora was perched on top of a large rock, gazing into the surrounding woods while Bow, the princesses, and Swift Wind peace-fully slept around the fire. Her Horde training ran through her mind, and she could hear Commander

Cobalt's voice in her memory: *When you're keeping watch, do it W-E-L-L!*

W: Wait patiently at your post until you are relieved. Don't wander off.

E: Empty your mind. Don't let your mind wander, either.

L: Look for lights or movements in the trees. Keep your eyes on your surroundings.

L: Listen for unusual sounds.

She had to admit that her Horde training still came in handy. Horde soldiers didn't have magical powers like the princesses did, but they were a skilled fighting force, and Adora had been one of their best.

She glanced at the campfire.

It's a good thing we're not being followed, she thought absently. *That campfire would definitely give away our location.*

That thought made her sit upright. She hadn't been acting like a Horde soldier on this journey.

They had made no effort to cover their tracks. Before going to bed, they'd been talking loudly. She was sure their voices must have carried through the woods. And now this fire—the smoke could probably be seen for miles.

She scanned the woods all around her, listening and focusing carefully.

Flash! She saw lights shine in the forest. Two small lights, one blue and one yellow. Adora blinked, and they disappeared.

Blue and yellow. *Like Catra's eyes,* Adora thought, *but they couldn't be, could they?* There was no way Catra could have known about this mission they were on. Adora hadn't noticed any signs of them being followed, though they could have been more careful . . .

"I must be seeing things," she muttered hopefully, trying to convince herself, and then she yawned. "Time to wake up Bow."

CHAPTER 5
ACROSS THE ICE BRIDGE

"No way. Seals are not cuter than penguins," Frosta was arguing.

"Of course they are," Mermista said. "They can bark and clap their flippers together. What's cuter than that?"

It was the next morning, and the travelers had returned to their path shortly after sunup. They had emerged from the woods and were walking across the rocky foothills of a low mountain range.

Now it was almost noon, and they were struggling for ways to pass the time. Frosta and Mermista had been debating about cute animals for the last hour. Bow had started counting his steps.

"Four thousand fifty-eight, four thousand fifty-nine . . ."

Perfuma was walking with her eyes half-closed and a peaceful smile on her face. Adora was shocked that she didn't bump into anything.

Adora and Glimmer were walking side by side, talking. They hadn't been friends for very long, and they still had a lot to learn about each other. Glimmer always had questions about the Horde.

"So Catra is a force captain. And now she's always with Scorpia, who has white hair and those big claw thingies, right? Is she a force captain, too?" Glimmer asked.

"I think she calls them pincers, actually, but yes, Scorpia is a force captain, too," Adora said. "Being made force captain is a pretty big deal when you're a Horde soldier."

Glimmer nodded. "I get it. Every time I think about you almost being one, I realize how lucky we are that you're on our side."

Adora smiled. "I'm just lucky that you and Bow were in the woods that day."

In front of them, Mermista and Frosta were still arguing.

"Penguins look like they're wearing clothes," Frosta countered, turning to face Mermista. "And they waddle!"

Frosta began to waddle like a penguin, still walking backward. Suddenly, Mermista reached out and grabbed her.

"Careful!" she warned.

They had come to a gorge—a narrow valley between the two hills. Frosta had almost tumbled backward into it.

"This isn't on the map," Bow said, frowning as he studied his tracker pad. "Sorry. I would have warned everyone."

"No big deal," Frosta said. She faced the gorge and held out her arms.

Whoosh! A stream of ice shot from her hands, stretching from one side to the other. It formed a bridge of ice about four feet wide.

"Instant ice bridge!" Frosta said proudly.

"Looks slippery," Glimmer said, and she transported across it in a shower of sparkles.

"Good idea," Swift Wind said, and he flew to the other side.

Frosta stepped onto the bridge and jumped in place. "Nice and sturdy. Come on!"

She made her way across the bridge, followed by Adora, Mermista, and Bow. They were about half-way across when an eerie sound filled the air.

Aaaaiiiiieeeeeeeee!

An enormous blue worm emerged from the bottom of the gorge. Its huge mouth was open, and four blue eyes glowed at the top of its head.

"An Elemental!" Glimmer cried.

The creature thrashed, whacking into the ice bridge. A crack zigzagged across it with lightning speed.

"Adora, we could use She-Ra right now," Bow said.

"On it!" Adora replied. She reached for her sword and held it up.

"For the honor—"

Whap! A rock struck the sword, sending it flying out of Adora's hand. Startled, Adora looked back at the other side of the gorge . . . to see Catra and Scorpia standing there!

"Hey, Adora," Catra said with a wicked grin.

CHAPTER 6
BATTLE ON THE GORGE

"Catra!" Adora cried. Then she realized—her sword!

Poof! Glimmer transported, caught the sword in midair, and landed on the ice bridge next to Adora.

Aaaaiiiiieeeeeeee! The Elemental lunged at them, its mouth open wide. Adora and Glimmer jumped to the side. Catra charged across the bridge with a determined gleam in her eye.

Adora held her sword over her head.

"For the honor of Grayskull!" she cried.

The sword began to shine with white light that surrounded Adora and lifted her up into the air.

Pink-and-purple light swirled around her, and a flame-like glow began to spread from her feet up to the ends of her hair.

She became taller and stronger. A white battle costume replaced her usual clothing, and a gold, winged helmet appeared on top of her mane of long, flowing golden hair. The glow faded as she floated gently back down on the bridge, transformed.

The Elemental immediately calmed down. It stopped attacking them, and then slowly sank down into the depths of the gorge. She-Ra's presence always turned off whatever internal switch made those monsters attack. But she still had another problem.

"One move, and Scorpia snaps your friend in half," Catra threatened.

Adora spun around. Scorpia had Bow in a head-lock, wrapped in her giant pincers.

"Sorry," Bow said.

Poof! Glimmer transported quickly and appeared behind Scorpia. She hit her with a sharp kick behind the knees. Startled, Scorpia let go of Bow. He quickly regrouped and aimed one of his arrows at Scorpia.

"Not this time," he said, and Scorpia raised both arms.

Whoosh! He shot an arrow at Scorpia. A net popped out of the base of the arrow, entangling her.

"*Aaaargh!*" Catra charged across the bridge toward She-Ra.

"Don't do it, Catra," She-Ra warned. "It's a long drop to the bottom of that gorge."

"I'm not gonna fall," Catra growled. "I couldn't finish things in Bright Moon, Adora. But I'm going to finish it now!"

She leapt at She-Ra, her claws extended. She-Ra lunged forward, sword extended. But the ice cracked under her feet, and she stumbled.

Catra was on her, and suddenly she wasn't.

She-Ra sat up to see Catra sprawled on the bridge, surrounded by chunks of ice.

"*Ice* to see you, Catra!" Frosta taunted.

The young princess was flying overhead on Swift Wind's back. "I call that one the Ice Blast," Frosta said with a proud grin.

She-Ra jumped to her feet. The ice bridge began to crack and groan.

"Glimmer, do you have one more in you?" She-Ra called out.

"Got it!" Glimmer cried. She ran to Bow and hugged him. Then she transported them both to the other side of the gorge.

Scorpia, meanwhile, had torn through her net and was making a beeline back to land. Catra threw off the ice chunks pinning her to the bridge.

The ice under She-Ra's feet shook violently, and she knew the bridge wasn't going to last. She reached down and grabbed Catra.

"Looks like you're not finishing anything today," She-Ra said. She tossed Catra to safety at the start of the bridge. Then she ran toward the other side. As the ice crumbled beneath her feet, she launched into a massive leap, landing on the other side of the gorge in a somersault. Then she transformed back into Adora.

Swift Wind landed nearby, and Frosta climbed off his back.

"Nice job, Swift Wind!" Frosta told him.

"You too, Ice Princess!" Swift Wind replied.

Wait, did he just give her a nickname? Are they bonding? *Seriously?* Adora wondered. But so much was happening that she didn't have time to dwell on it.

Across the gorge, Catra and Scorpia were already out of sight.

"What was that about?" Bow asked.

"They must have been following us this whole

time," Adora said, shaking her head. "I can't believe I didn't realize it. I guess she thought I'd be vulnerable if she attacked me away from the kingdom."

"Catra is, like, obsessed with you," Mermista said.

"Well, we sent her packing—again," Glimmer said. "Although I used up a lot of my powers just now."

"You did great, Glimmer!" Perfuma said. "I would have jumped in, but you all seemed like you had it under control."

Mermista nodded. "Yeah. There were only, like, two of them, anyway."

"Did you see me pummel Catra with that ice blast?" Frosta asked, punching the air. *"Bam!* Me and Swifty were right there!"

"Yeah, thanks," Adora said, but she felt a pang of jealousy at the sound of another nickname.

Bow peered down into the gorge. "Looks like

you calmed down that Elemental. I wonder what kind of First Ones site is down there."

Adora followed his gaze. "Maybe some kind of research outpost?"

"By the way, why didn't you let the Elemental keep Catra busy?" Glimmer asked. "We could have escaped while she was fighting it."

Adora knew the answer to that question was complicated. Until recently, Catra had been her best friend. And Adora still had hope—even if it was a small hope—that Catra could be saved someday. She wasn't ready to leave Catra in the clutches of a monstrous creature.

"She won't bother us again," Adora replied.

"We should be close to the lake now, shouldn't we?" Perfuma asked.

Bow looked at the map on his tracker pad. "We're not too far," he said. "I'll lead the way."

Adora felt shaken as she headed down the path.

She had told Glimmer that Catra wouldn't bother them again, but she knew that wasn't true. The question was, when would it happen next? And how many Horde troops would Catra have with her next time?

CHAPTER 7
ARCANA ISLAND

"I see water!" Mermista called out.

It had been nearly an hour since they'd left the gorge and followed the path down the mountainside. They had reached another forest, and over the last mile, the trees had begun to thin out. Now they could see a blue lake sparkling ahead of them.

"Did we ever come up with a plan for how we're going to get to the island in the middle of the lake?" Bow asked.

"Swift Wind can give everybody a ride!" Frosta suggested.

"Hold on there, now. I am not some kind of mass-transportation vehicle. I am a magnificent winged horse!" Swift Wind said.

"Well, if you took two of us at a time, that might be the best way to get to the island," Adora said. "And you could still do that, you know, magnificently."

Mermista interrupted. "Um, I can totally swim there."

Swift Wind challenged Adora. "I thought you said that walking was better than flying."

"Well, sure, but we can't walk on water," Adora replied. "We need a boat."

"You mean like that one?" Perfuma asked, pointing.

A white, flat-bottomed boat sat on the sandy shore of the peaceful lake. When they reached it, they found oars tucked inside.

"It's big enough for all of us!" Frosta said. "We're in luck!"

"It's like it was put here just for us," Perfuma added.

Adora frowned. "It's too convenient. Is it a trap?"

"Not everything is a trap, Adora," Glimmer said. "And even if it is, we have to find out. How else are we going to get to the island?"

Adora nodded. "You're right," she said. "Let's go!"

They dragged the boat to the edge of the water and boarded it—even Swift Wind. Then the princesses and Bow picked up oars, and they glided out onto the lake.

"The water is such a beautiful shade of blue!" Perfuma remarked.

Mermista dipped a hand in the lake. "This water feels . . . I don't know, charged or something. Magical."

"I can feel it, too," Frosta said in a loud whisper.

"Then we must be in the right place," Bow said.

They rowed in silence for a while, until the forest disappeared on the horizon. Adora spotted something shimmering up ahead.

"What is that?" she wondered out loud.

"It looks like . . . some kind of a shield, maybe," Bow guessed.

"I think you're right," Adora agreed.

A tall, shimmering wall rose up out of the water in the middle of the lake. It towered above them and seemed to be in the shape of an enclosed pen.

"I bet it protects the island!" Frosta said.

As they got closer, Adora realized something.

"It's a hologram," she said. "And it's covered with First Ones writing. Let me translate."

Slowly, she read the words on the wall out loud.

"'Arcana Island is a sanctuary for rare, magical creatures,'" she began. "'They once roamed free on Etheria, but we moved them here to protect them from evil forces.'"

"What kind of evil forces?" Glimmer asked.

Adora shook her head. "It doesn't say."

"'To enter, speak the password,'" Adora continued reading. "'And treat all creatures on this island with respect.'"

"What's the password?" Frosta asked.

Adora scanned the gate. "Truculenter," she said.

The holographic gate sizzled, and an archway opened up in the wall in front of them. They rowed through it, and an island spread out before them. It was covered with green trees and colorful flowers. Birds flew among the trees, and a mix of furry, scaly, and prickly creatures scampered on its shores.

"Wow!" Frosta exclaimed. "It's the Island of Magical Creatures!"

CHAPTER 8
TWINKLES THE MIGHTY

They brought the boat to shore and stepped onto the island.

Perfuma clapped her hands together. "It's so beautiful here!" she exclaimed.

"Look at all the magical creatures!" Frosta said.

"They don't look magical to me," Swift Wind remarked. "They look like regular creatures."

"I don't think the First Ones would have protected the island like they did if they weren't special," Adora said.

"We should talk to them," Glimmer suggested.

"Do you think they talk?" Bow asked.

"They might, if they're magical," she replied.

"There's one way to find out," Adora said. She turned to the nearest animal—a little black-and-white creature digging in the dirt. "Hey there. Can you talk?"

The animal stopped digging and turned around. She lifted up her tail.

"Watch out!" Glimmer warned, pulling Adora away. "That's a skunk! They're cute but they have this really stinky spray . . ."

She was too late. A mist shot out from under the skunk's tail.

"Aaaaaaaaahhhhhhh!" everyone screamed.

Then Perfuma sniffed the air. "Wait," she said. "That smells like . . . flowers!"

The skunk turned around and beamed at Perfuma. Then she trotted over to Perfuma and nuzzled her head against her ankles. Perfuma picked her up.

"What a cutie you are," she said. "And you smell so nice!"

"Wait a second," Glimmer said. "Is that the skunk's magic power? Its spray smells like flowers?"

"I think that's a lovely power," Perfuma said.

"Maybe, but, like, how would that help us fight the Horde exactly?" Mermista asked. "Unless, I guess, they smell bad."

"The Fright Zone does smell like burning garbage, mostly," Adora admitted. "But I see your point. These animals might not have the skills we need."

"There's got to be some that talk," Frosta insisted. She cupped her hands around her mouth. "Can any of you magical creatures talk?" she yelled.

The animals stopped flying and scampering. One of them, a hedgehog, scurried toward Frosta and made chattering noises.

Frosta sighed. "That's not very helpful."

Swift Wind stepped forward. "I speak hedge-hog," he said.

Adora raised an eyebrow. "You do?"

"Hedgehog, squirrel, and cow," Swift Wind replied. "Oh, and pig and dog. But that's about it."

"Very impressive," Bow said.

"Just don't ask me to speak raccoon," Swift Wind said. "Their language makes no sense at all. It's mostly just laughing and burping."

"So what is the hedgehog saying?" Frosta asked.

The hedgehog seemed to understand Frosta and began chattering again. Swift Wind nodded his head, listening.

"He says that he is Twinkles the Mighty, the leader of this island, and he demands to know why we are intruding," Swift Wind translated.

"Twinkles the Mighty?" Glimmer repeated, looking down at the fuzzy little creature.

"Well, he is mighty cute," Perfuma said.

The little hedgehog started to spin around in a circle. He spun and spun . . . and with each spin, he got bigger.

"What is happening here?" Bow asked.

Twinkles kept spinning . . . and spinning . . . and spinning . . . until soon a hedgehog the size of an elephant stood in front of them.

"Yes!" Frosta cheered.

Adora stepped forward and gave an awkward bow. "Greetings, um, mighty leader of this island. Are all of the creatures here like you?"

The hedgehog spun in circles again, returning to his normal size. Then he started chattering again.

"He says that before he answers your questions, you need to answer his," Swift Wind said. "Who are you and why are you here?"

"We are princesses of Etheria, except for Bow and Swift Wind here," Adora replied. "We're all members of the Rebellion against an evil force called the Horde. And we've come to ask for your help."

Twinkles fell on his back and started laughing in a high, squeaky voice. He kicked his tiny legs.

"What's so funny?" Adora asked.

Twinkles jumped up and spoke to Swift Wind.

"He says that the island was created to *protect* these animals from evil," Swift Wind translated. "They are peaceful creatures. How can *they* help you?"

Frosta spoke up. "Because you're magic, and that's one thing the Horde doesn't have," she said. "You can use your powers to help us save Etheria."

The other animals behind Twinkles began to speak up in a chorus of chirps, squeaks, and roars. Twinkles let out a high-pitched squeak and they all quieted down. Then he addressed Swift Wind.

"He says that the animals are all excited to meet the princesses," Swift Wind reported. "And some of them want to help. They need to hold a council to decide. But first, he'll let some of them show off their powers."

Frosta nudged Glimmer. "This is going to be awesome."

A golden mountain lion with green eyes pad-ded up to the group of animals. Twinkles said something.

"This is Mehira," Swift Wind translated.

Mehira nodded to Twinkles, and then she took off running. She ran in circles around the princesses and Bow, speeding so fast that she was just a blur. Then she stopped instantly in front of Twinkles.

"Wow! That was fast!" Glimmer exclaimed.

Adora nodded, wide-eyed. She had never seen a mountain lion before—or many of the animals gathered behind Twinkles. The villages around Bright Moon had mostly squirrels, horses, cows, pigs, and pets like cats and dogs.

They all look magical to me, she realized. *With or without special powers!*

Next, a porcupine waddled up.

"This is Winda," Swift Wind explained, translating for Twinkles.

Winda jumped up and performed what looked

like a martial-arts kick with her short back legs. As she landed, sharp quills flew out of her back. They landed in a tree about fifteen feet behind her, forming a perfect circle.

"Now that is accurate!" Bow said. "I wish I could shoot arrows that fast."

After Winda came Tajana, a white fox. She blinked her green eyes—and turned completely invisible. Then she moved toward Frosta and nuzzled against her leg.

"It's so cool! I can feel her, but I can't see her!" Frosta exclaimed. "She would make an excellent spy."

"Sure," Swift Wind said. "But can she fly, or talk? Can any of these guys? The answer is one big *naaaaaaaaay*."

Then a young deer stepped up. His antlers were just beginning to sprout. Twinkles introduced him.

"This is Treeleaf," Swift Wind translated.

Adora stared at Treeleaf. Next to Swift Wind, the deer was the most beautiful creature she had ever seen, with his golden-brown fur and deep, dark eyes.

"Treeleaf," Adora repeated.

The deer closed his eyes, and his body glowed with a soft light. His fur turned from brown to pink. Then orange. Then yellow. Then green. Then blue. Then purple, and finally back to brown.

"Wow, that was beautiful!" Adora remarked.

Swift Wind snorted. "Big deal. I've got rainbow wings! All the colors, all the time."

Treeleaf rejoined the other animals, and nobody else stepped forward.

"Thank you, Twinkles," Adora said. "Now maybe we can—"

Twinkles interrupted her.

"He says there's one more," Swift Wind said.

The animals parted a little bit as a sloth slowly crawled up to the princesses.

"What is that?" Adora asked.

"It's a sloth," Swift Wind replied, and then he listened to the hedgehog. "His name is Felix."

"What does he do, besides being totally adorable?" Mermista wanted to know.

Twinkles chattered again.

"Twinkles says, 'Wait for it,'" Swift Wind replied.

So they waited, their eyes on the sloth. Then Felix slowly began to float up off the ground. When he was about a foot in the air, he stopped and hovered there.

Twinkles squeaked.

"That roughly translates to 'ta-da'!" Swift Wind said.

"He can fly!" Frosta exclaimed.

"That's not flying," Swift Wind pointed out. "He's not even moving. He's just floating there."

"But he's above the ground," Perfuma pointed out. "Isn't that the same as flying?"

"Absolutely not!" Swift Wind snorted. "Flying is

soaring through the air on majestic wings." He flapped his own wings for emphasis.

"Swift Wind is right," Adora said, and Swift Wind beamed at her. "He is the only creature on Etheria that can fly. Well, except I guess for birds. And what are those bugs with the orange wings?"

"Butterflies," Bow answered.

"Right, butterflies!" Adora said. "They fly. And so do those black-and-yellow things that sting you . . ."

"I know I'm not the only *flying* animal on Etheria," Swift Wind interrupted her, and he sounded annoyed. "But I am the only *magical* flying animal."

You blew it again, Adora, she scolded herself. *Why do I always say the wrong thing to Swift Wind?*

"Flying. Floating. Whatever," Mermista said. "This furry guy is pretty cute."

Felix very slowly broke into a smile.

"Twinkles says that all of the other animals have powers, too," Swift Wind reported. "But these are some of the strongest ones."

"These are awesome!" Frosta cried. "I want Tajana to be my magical creature sidekick. We could go on super-secret spy missions together."

Twinkles chattered to Swift Wind.

"Twinkles wants you to know that not all of the animals have such strong powers," Swift Wind translated. "Most of them are like the skunk or the sloth. Or that bunny."

He nodded toward a cute little rabbit who hopped forward. He burped, and rainbow-colored bubbles streamed from his mouth.

"Most are quite helpless and vulnerable, which is why they need protection," Swift Wind added.

Glimmer leaned toward Adora. "This isn't exactly what we were expecting, but I definitely think there are some useful powers here," she said. "Although none of them are as amazing as Swift Wind, right?"

Adora wasn't listening. She was staring at Treeleaf, who kept changing from one color to the next.

Twinkles clapped his two front feet together and squeaked.

"He is calling a meeting of the Animal Council tonight," Swift Wind said. "He welcomes us to enjoy the island while we wait for them to come to a decision. The animals would like to get the chance to know you better before they decide. If you ask me, though, they're just being difficult."

"No, it's okay," Adora said. "It will be dark soon, and we need to stay on the island tonight anyway."

"It's a plan, then," Glimmer agreed. "I just wonder if the animals will decide to help us . . ."

CHAPTER 9
FOLLOWING TREELEAF

Adora and Swift Wind took in the scene as the others started to get to know the animals.

Frosta had taught Tajana, the white fox, how to play hide-and-seek. She chased the playful fox, who kept appearing and disappearing.

Mermista was chilling on a hammock strung between two trees, with Felix the sloth floating in the air next to her.

Perfuma and the skunk, whose name was Lily, were walking around the edge of the woods, sniffing the colorful flowers.

Glimmer was using Bow's tracker pad to time the speed of Mehira the mountain lion.

And Bow had created a target out of some driftwood and was taking turns shooting at it with Winda the porcupine.

"This is actually pretty incredible," Swift Wind told Adora. "I mean, some of their powers might be a little weird, and they're obviously not as good as mine. But these are definitely not ordinary creatures. I'm not alone!"

"Is that what it felt like after I transformed you?" Adora asked. "Like you were all alone in the world?"

"Well, at first none of the other horses would even talk to me," he said. "That hurt. But then I joined the Rebellion, and I felt like I was a part of something bigger than myself, you know? So then I didn't feel so alone."

He's opening up to me, Adora realized, and she planned her next words carefully. "I understand," she said. "And I know what happened to you was an accident, Swift Wind, but I'm really glad you're part of the Rebellion. We wouldn't—"

Treeleaf approached them, and she stopped. The deer's fur was a beautiful, deep purple color. He nodded with his head toward the woods.

"You want me to follow you?" Adora asked.

Treeleaf nodded.

"Okay," Adora said, and she walked toward him.

"I'm pretty sure he wants *us* to follow him," Swift Wind said, trotting after them. "I mean, I don't speak deer, but that's what it felt like to me."

He followed Adora and Treeleaf into the woods. The air felt cool under the canopy of the green trees, and leaves crunched underneath their feet. Birds darted between the tree branches. A turtle ambled across the path. More bunnies munched on plants, burping rainbow bubbles. Squirrels and chipmunks scampered up the tree trunks as they walked by.

"There are animals all over this island," Adora remarked.

Swift Wind stopped. "Hmm. I wonder if those are ordinary squirrels, or if they have powers?" he asked. "I could talk to them and find out. Adora, what do you think?"

But Adora, transfixed by the deer, wasn't listening. Swift Wind snorted and continued on behind them. Nearby, two of the squirrels ran down the tree trunk. One of them picked up a rock ten times her size and held it over her head while the other squirrel gathered the nuts hidden underneath.

"Hey, where are we going?" Swift Wind asked Adora. "I mean, I don't speak deer but I could try."

Treeleaf was silent. Adora shrugged, and they all kept walking. They came to a bubbling brook. A family of ducks was floating downstream, quacking to each other.

Quack! Quack! Quack!

Adora's eyes lit up. "That sounds like . . . quack!" she cried. "These must be ducks, right? 'Does a duck quack?' I get it now!"

Swift Wind grinned. "I knew you would."

Treeleaf gracefully leapt and landed on a rock in the middle of the brook. Then he jumped to the other side.

"No problem for me, either," Swift Wind said. "I can do this!"

He took off, flapping his wings. But as he soared above the brook, his head bumped into an over-hanging tree branch. He tumbled down and landed in the water with a splash.

"That tree branch came out of nowhere!" he sputtered. Then he climbed up onto the banks. "Need help, Adora? I can fly over there and get you."

"Better not," Adora replied. "I've got it."

She imitated Treeleaf, jumping to the rock in the middle of the brook, and then taking one more jump onto the forest floor.

"Thanks, Treeleaf," Adora said, patting the deer's head.

"Treeleaf, Treeleaf, Treeleaf," Swift Wind muttered under his breath.

"Did you say something?" Adora asked.

"Uh, just, 'Treeleaf, lead the way'!" Swift Wind replied.

They continued on a mossy path that led to a cave carved out of a low boulder. Treeleaf motioned for them to follow him inside.

"It could be a trap," Swift Wind warned.

"Treeleaf wouldn't do that," Adora said, and she followed him inside.

It was dark in the cave, but her sword began to glow right away, lighting up the space. On the walls she could see more paintings like the ones in the ruins outside Bright Moon.

These paintings showed First Ones interacting with the animals of the island. The images reminded Adora of her friends and the animals they had connected with. One woman was racing a mountain lion, and another one was having target practice with a porcupine, just like Bow and Winda.

"I see," Adora said. "There used to be people on this island."

Treeleaf nodded.

Swift Wind interjected. "Twinkles told me that the very first animals here lived with people, and they were all friends," he said. "Then the people left, and the animals were very sad. The animals have been waiting for people to return for a very long time."

"Then maybe the animals will vote to come with us," Adora went on. "Although I guess the First Ones must have had a good reason for keeping them safe here. Maybe we can ask Twinkles."

"You mean maybe *I* should ask Twinkles," Swift Wind said.

"Right," Adora said.

Treeleaf moved over to a picture on the wall and stopped. There was a picture of a deer running through the forest and a woman with long hair flowing behind her.

Adora smiled. "That could be you and me," she said, and Treeleaf nodded.

"Oh, please," Swift Wind said, rolling his eyes. "Is that really why we came all this way?"

"Whatever your council decides, we'll accept it," Adora told Treeleaf. "And even if you decide to stay here, we'll come back and visit. You shouldn't be alone forever."

"Okay, it's going to be dark soon," Swift Wind piped up. "We'd better get back."

Treeleaf lowered his head and nudged Adora with his antlers. She stroked the fur on his head.

Swift Wind snorted. "Fine. I'll find my own way back. I'm sure you'll be fine with your new friend, Treeleaf." Then he turned and left the cave.

"What's the matter with him?" Adora wondered out loud, and then it hit her: He was jealous!

She shook her head. Swift Wind could be so confusing! She'd been trying so hard to make a connection with him, and he hadn't even noticed. But the minute Treeleaf had shown up, he was jealous.

He is being so silly! Adora thought with a sigh. *Doesn't he realize that I think he's awesome? That there's no better companion for She-Ra?*

Adora and Treeleaf left the cave and made their way through the woods as the setting sun cast an orange glow on the forest floor. Twinkles and Swift Wind were waiting for them when they got back. If Swift Wind was embarrassed by his jealous behavior in the forest, he wasn't showing it, Adora observed.

"Twinkles says that we should enjoy the feast they have prepared for us while they have their council," Swift Wind reported.

Twinkles nodded, and then he and all the animals disappeared into the forest.

"Okay, where's the feast?" Glimmer asked.

Perfuma pointed to a long, flat rock. "I think this must be it."

They gathered around the rock, which was strewn with leaves, flowers, nuts, and berries.

"That looks delicious!" Perfuma remarked.

"That is literally rabbit food," Mermista replied.

"Well, it was nice of them to do this for us," Frosta remarked.

"We've still got some rations," Adora said. "I'll get a fire going. We should eat and then set up for the night."

"How long do you think their meeting will take?" Frosta asked.

"Probably not too long," Glimmer guessed.

But the sun set, and the animals didn't return. The group talked around the fire for a while, chatting about the island. Then everyone started to yawn.

"Aren't they done yet?" Frosta asked sleepily, leaning against Glimmer's shoulder.

"I'm sure they'll be done soon," Adora replied, her eyes drooping.

A thought crossed her mind that they should have someone keep watch, but she was sure they would all stay awake until the animals finished with their meeting. But the animals still didn't return, and one by one the rebels fell asleep. Only Swift Wind and Adora remained awake, but then Swift Wind started to snore, and Adora soon drifted off.

She dreamed of running through the woods with Treeleaf, with her hair down and flowing behind her. They emerged from the forest into a beautiful clearing and a sunny blue sky overhead. Swift Wind flew across the sky, and Adora stopped and waved to him. Then she glanced back into the woods and saw two eyes shining there, one blue and one yellow . . .

"Adora, wake up!"

Her eyes opened to see Swift Wind bending

over her. The sun was slowly rising, and Twinkles was next to him, riding on Mehira's back.

"Twinkles says that intruders are coming to the island!" Swift Wind said. "And they're *not* princesses."

Adora bolted upright. "Catra!"

CHAPTER 10
CATRA'S BACK!

"Everyone, wake up!" Adora yelled.

Frosta jumped up. "What is it?"

Perfuma sat up, stretching. Mermista yawned. Bow started shaking Glimmer awake.

"What?" Glimmer groaned.

"Catra's on her way," Adora said. "At least, I think so. Twinkles, how many intruders are there? And is one of them a girl with eyes like a cat and claws?"

Twinkles chattered away.

"He says there are a dozen soldiers and six machine animals," Swift Wind translated. "And there is a cat-eyed girl, with someone who looks like a crab."

"A scorpion actually. That's Scorpia," Adora said.

"And the machine animals he's talking about must be Horde robots. They look like spiders."

"Are they on the island yet?" Glimmer asked.

Twinkles shook his head.

"Then take us to the highest point on the island," Adora said. "Somewhere we can see them but they can't see us."

Twinkles and the mountain lion took off, but traveled slowly enough for the others to keep up. They stopped at the top of a tree-covered hill.

"Stay behind the trees," Adora warned. She pushed aside some leaves and looked out.

Several Horde skiffs were flying above the lake, heading toward the island. The lead skiff held Catra and Scorpia. The rest held Horde soldiers in gray uniforms, their faces masked by helmets. Some of the skiffs towed platforms carrying robots—but not the spiderlike Horde robots that Adora knew. These robots looked like machine animals, just as

Twinkles had reported. There was a lion, a bear, a horse, and an alligator.

"What?" Adora muttered. She'd never seen robots like that in the Fright Zone before.

But there was no time to ponder where they'd come from. Catra and her troops were advancing fast.

"This is the Horde that I was telling you about," Adora told Twinkles. "This is our fault. They followed us here. But we'll protect you."

"That's right!" Glimmer echoed.

Twinkles didn't reply. He tapped Mehira, and the mountain lion took off down the hill at super speed.

"Where are they going?" Frosta wondered.

"Probably getting the animals to safety," Adora replied. "Swift Wind, can you go follow them? Make sure everyone's okay?"

Swift Wind nodded. "Got it!" he said, and he galloped off.

Adora turned to her friends. "Look, we're out-numbered, but we can do this."

She held up her sword. "For the honor of Grayskull!"

Adora transformed into She-Ra. Then she charged down the hill, followed by Glimmer, Bow, Frosta, Perfuma, and Mermista.

They broke through the tree line as the skiffs landed on shore. The rebels didn't wait for the Horde to disembark. They launched into an attack.

Mermista called up a powerful wave from the lake. *Whoosh!* It slammed into a skiff carrying two Horde soldiers, pulling them back into the lake.

Wham! Frosta shot an ice blast at a Horde soldier, knocking him into the sand.

Zap! Bow shot an electric arrow into a skiff, shorting it out. The Horde soldiers jumped out of their seats to escape the sizzling metal.

Whap! Perfuma hit one of the soldiers with a

whiplike vine. It wrapped around her and knocked her off the skiff.

She-Ra and Glimmer charged at Catra and Scorpia. Glimmer lobbed sparkle bombs at them, and they dove off their skiffs. She-Ra ran to Catra and rested the tip of her sword on Catra's chest.

"How did you get in here?" She-Ra asked.

Catra grinned. "I sent a spy bot ahead to follow you. That's how I got the password to the gate."

"Spy bot?" She-Ra asked.

Catra snapped her fingers and a tiny orb-shaped bot flew off the skiff and hovered next to her. Its eye, a camera lens, rotated back and forth.

"That's new," She-Ra said. She nodded to the animal robots. "And so are they. And you somehow figured out how to attack the Moonstone of Bright Moon. Where is all this new technology coming from? Hordak?"

"Let's just say we've got a secret weapon now, Adora," Catra said. Then she whistled.

The lion robot came to life, its eyes glowing red. It leapt off the skiff and slammed into She-Ra, knocking her off Catra.

"Good kitty!" Catra said.

Grunting, She-Ra pushed off the heavy metal creature. The robot lion growled and pounced again.

Adora dodged and swung her sword at the lion, but the robot leapt, and she missed it. Then . . . *wham!* Something smacked into the back of her knees, and she stumbled forward.

Looking back, she saw the robot bear standing over her, growling. She jumped to her feet. The robot alligator had joined the other two robots, its mechanical jaws snapping. The three creatures had her cornered. She swung in a circle, sword extended, and both creatures stepped back.

Catra jumped up on a rock and watched the scene, her hands on her hips.

"Now it's my turn to ask you some questions, Adora," Catra said. "Where is it?"

"Where's what?" She-Ra asked, not taking her eyes off the robots.

"Where's the First Ones tech you came here for?" Catra asked.

Catra doesn't know about the animals, She-Ra realized. *She thinks we're here to find tech.*

"What makes you think I'd tell you?" She-Ra asked.

Catra held up a small remote control. "Because just one push of a button and these robots will blow. And I don't think even She-Ra is fireproof."

She-Ra knew from the gleam in Catra's eyes that she wasn't kidding.

"There's nothing here," She-Ra lied. "We were following a lead, and it didn't turn up anything."

"I know when you're lying, Adora," Catra shot back. "Now tell me—where's the tech?"

She-Ra thought quickly. From the corner of her

eyes, she could see her friends still battling Scorpia and the Horde soldiers. They were too busy to know what Catra was up to. If only she could get that remote away from her . . .

"Hey!" Catra cried.

The remote control seemed to magically disappear from Catra's hands. She-Ra blinked—and then saw the white fox materializing as she ran into the woods with the remote in her mouth.

She-Ra was grateful—but terrified at the same time. If Catra knew about the animals . . .

"What's happening is that you lose again, Catra," She-Ra said.

She spun around, driving her sword into the robot lion. The robot sizzled, and the bear and alligator charged at her. At the same time . . .

"Chaaaaaaaarge!"

Swift Wind emerged from the woods, followed by Mehira, a bunch of ninja porcupines, and a ten-foot-tall hedgehog.

Catra's eyes widened. "What the—ow!" she cried, as porcupine needles landed in her arm like darts.

Twinkles stomped on the robot alligator, crushing it to bits with his giant, cute feet.

Swift Wind kicked the bear robot, knocking it on its back. She-Ra spun around and thrust her sword through the robot, finishing it.

Mehira, meanwhile, ran circles around the remaining Horde soldiers, pushing them closer and closer together. Perfuma lassoed them with one of her plant vines.

"I don't know what's going on here, but I know it's big," Catra said. "We might not win today, Adora, but we'll be back! We'll be back with more soldiers and more robots, and we'll take this island!"

"Oh, be quiet!"

Frosta ran up, glaring at Catra. She hit her with an ice blast, freezing her in place.

She-Ra gazed around. The animal robots were sparking piles of junk; the skiffs were all disabled, and

Scorpia and the Horde soldiers were either tied up in Perfuma's vines or trapped in one of Bow's nets.

"Well, we took care of them," Glimmer remarked. "What now?"

She-Ra frowned. "I don't know. If we send them back, they'll only return."

Twinkles spun in a circle, returning to his normal size. Then he spoke to Swift Wind.

"Twinkles says to stand back," Swift Wind translated. "Treeleaf has a power that can help us."

The princesses and Bow obeyed. Treeleaf stepped out of the forest. He lowered his head, and streams of light flowed from his antlers.

The light touched the heads of Catra, Scorpia, and all of the Horde soldiers. Their eyes closed and their heads drooped.

"What is he doing?" She-Ra asked.

"Twinkles says they'll be asleep for a little while," Swift Wind answered. "And when they wake up, they won't remember the last twenty-four hours."

"Wow . . . that's a pretty specific power," Mermista said.

"It's exactly the power we need," She-Ra said. "Now we just have to get them off the island."

"On it," Mermista replied. She held out her arms, and an enormous wave rose out of the lake. She lowered her arms, and the wave dropped to the shore and picked up Catra, Scorpia, and the Horde. Then it carried them away.

"They'll wake up on the other side of the lake," Mermista said.

"That should be good enough," Glimmer guessed.

She-Ra turned to the animals. "Thank you," she said, and Twinkles began to chatter.

"We did what we could to protect our island," Swift Wind translated for him. "And now, we are ready to give you our decision. We will leave this island and help you defeat the Horde!"

CHAPTER 11
DECISIONS

She-Ra transformed back into Adora. She looked at Glimmer.

"You don't look happy about this news," Glimmer said.

Adora frowned. "It's just—"

"I know what Adora is thinking," Swift Wind said. He turned to Twinkles. "You should stay here on the island."

Adora nodded. "That's exactly what I was thinking."

"But why? Isn't that why we came here?" Frosta asked.

"It is," Adora admitted. "And these animals are

amazing. They would be a great addition to the Rebellion."

"They would," Swift Wind agreed. "I know you sent me back there to protect them, Adora, but they were like an organized team of skilled warriors. They jumped into action to save the island—and to help you."

"That's exactly why they need to stay here," Adora said. She turned to the princesses and Bow. "Treeleaf took me into the woods. There are so many creatures in there! They're all magical, but not all of them can fight. They need protection. The animals should stay here and protect this place."

"And if you ever need help, you can call on us," Swift Wind added.

Twinkles nodded and answered him.

"Twinkles says you are right—they will stay," Swift Wind said. "But if you need their help, you can always come back."

"Before we go, there's something I'd like to do," Adora said. She turned to Bow. "Do you think you can help me change an ancient First Ones password?"

Bow grinned. "I'm not sure, but I'd like to try."

"We'll be back," Adora said. "Swift Wind, can you give us a lift?"

"Sure thing," Swift Wind said, and Adora and Bow climbed on his back. They flew back to the holographic barrier protecting the island.

"Just fly back and forth, if you don't mind," Adora instructed. "I'll try to see if I can find a password reset."

"Do you see the word 'settings' anywhere?" Bow asked.

"No," Adora replied. She scanned the symbols lighting up the wall. "But there is the word for *shield*. Maybe that's a security thing?"

"Try tapping it," Bow suggested.

"Swift Wind, get us closer, please," Adora said.

"I will, but only because you said *please*," Swift Wind replied.

They flew closer, and Adora reached out and tapped the word *shield*. Nothing happened.

"Hmm," Bow said. "Try using your sword."

Adora touched the wall with her sword. Again, nothing happened.

"Okay, now try touching it with your sword and saying the current password," Bow suggested.

Adora frowned. "What was it again? It was a weird word."

"Truculenter," Swift Wind reminded her.

"Right," Adora said. "Thanks, Swift Wind."

She tapped the wall again with her sword. "Truculenter!"

The word for *shield* disappeared, and an empty box appeared.

"You did it!" Bow said. "Now enter the new password."

"I can read First Ones language, but I'm still learning how to write it," Adora replied uncertainly.

"You can do it," Bow said. "Keep it simple."

Adora nodded and took a deep breath. With a sword, she drew a line from right to left across the box. Then she drew four symbols attached to the bottom of the line, from right to left.

When she was done, she tapped the box. It disappeared, and the word *shield* appeared.

"What did you change it to?" Bow asked.

"Treeleaf," Adora replied. "That's one I'm sure I'll never forget."

"Treeleaf—of course," Swift Wind muttered.

"Okay, thanks, Swift Wind!" Adora said. "Let's return to the island."

When they got back, they found the animals on the shore with the princesses, by the flat-bottomed boat.

"We changed the password on the wall," Adora told Twinkles. "You should be safe again."

Twinkles made some squeaky noises.

"He said *thank you*," Swift Wind reported. "And he wishes us a safe journey home."

"One thing before we go," Adora said, and she looked at Swift Wind. "If you want to stay here, with the animals, I understand."

CHAPTER 12
A BOND AT LAST?

"What are you saying?" Swift Wind asked Adora. "That you don't need me anymore?"

"No, of course not!" Adora replied. "I just want you to be happy. I know it's hard for you to be the only magical creature in Bright Moon. If you stayed here, you'd be with your own kind. And you'd make a great addition to their community."

"Is that what you really think?" Swift Wind asked. "Or do you want to leave me here and take Treeleaf with you?"

"No, of course not," Adora said. "You've got no reason to be jealous of Treeleaf, you know."

Swift Wind looked away from her. "Jealous? *Pffffftht!*"

"Okay, then you've got to believe me that I was only asking because I wanted you to be happy," Adora said. "The animals on this island are amazing, but none of them could take your place. You are as much a part of the Rebellion as any of us."

"Hmm," Swift Wind said, as though he still needed convincing.

Adora looked at him. "And you're the only magical creature I need," she said. "You were special to begin with, and She-Ra's sword only made you even more special. We're linked by the sword, Swift Wind. I can't be She-Ra without you."

"And I wouldn't be Swift Wind without you," he replied.

Adora looked into his blue eyes and smiled.

"Good," she said. "Now, try to stay *not* jealous for the next two minutes."

She walked over to Treeleaf and patted his neck. "I'm really glad that I met you," she said. "And when we defeat the Horde, and Etheria is safe again, we'll come back and visit. You won't be alone forever."

In response, Treeleaf changed his color to a deep, warm pink.

The others said goodbye to their new animal friends. Mermista hugged Felix the sloth. Glimmer stroked Mehira's fur. Frosta cuddled Tajana the white fox one last time. And Bow patted the porcupine very, very carefully.

Swift Wind nodded to Twinkles. "Goodbye, my mighty little friend," he said. "I wish you were coming with us. You'd make a great leader of the revolution!"

Then they boarded the boat and rowed away from the island.

"Well, that was some adventure," Glimmer remarked to Adora. "Even though it didn't turn out exactly the way we planned."

"I know," Adora replied, and then she lowered

her voice to a whisper. "But I really think I may have bonded with Swift Wind on this trip. Finally!"

When they reached the shore, they climbed off the boat.

"Guess it's time to start our long, long walk," Frosta said.

"Adora, you and Swift Wind should fly back to Bright Moon," Perfuma suggested. "We won't mind."

"That's okay," Adora said. "Princesses need to stick together, right?"

"You princesses can stick together," Swift Wind said, flapping his wings. "But this horse is flying home. See ya later!"

Then he took off into the sky.

Glimmer looked at Adora. "So you bonded, huh?"

Adora laughed. "Maybe not this time," she said. "But I have a feeling it will happen soon!"

ABOUT THE AUTHOR

Tracey West has written more than 300 books for children and young adults, including the following series: Pixie Tricks, Hiro's Quest, and Dragon Masters. She has appeared on the *New York Times* bestseller list as the author of the Pokémon chapter book adaptations. Tracey currently lives with her family in New York State's Catskill Mountains. She can be found on Twitter at @TraceyWestBooks.